JANE ASHER'S

CALENDAR
OF
CAKES

JANE ASHER'S

CALENDAR
OF
CAKES

PELHAM BOOKS
Stephen Greene Press

PELHAM BOOKS/STEPHEN GREENE PRESS

Published by the Penguin Group
27 Wrights Lane, London W8 5TZ, England
Viking Penguin Inc., 40 West 23rd Street, New York, New York 10010, USA
The Stephen Greene Press, 15, Muzzey Street, Lexington, Massachusetts
02173, U.S.A.
Penguin Books Australia Ltd, Ringwood, Victoria, Australia
Penguin Books Canada Ltd, 2801 John Street, Markham, Ontario, Canada L3R 1B4
Penguin Books (NZ) Ltd, 182–190 Wairau Road, Auckland 10, New Zealand

Penguin Books Ltd, Registered Offices: Harmondsworth, Middlesex, England

First published 1989

Typeset in Bembo by Goodfellow & Egan, Cambridge
Photographs by Chris Crofton
Diagrams by Gillie Newman
Colour reproduction by Anglia Graphics, Bedford
Printed and bound by Butler and Tanner, Frome, Somerset

ISBN 0 7207 1898 8
A CIP catalogue record for this book is available from the British Library.

CONTENTS

THE CAKES

January

February

March

April

May

June

July

August

September

October

November

December

INTRODUCTION

Every month of every year contains some special occasion to celebrate, and a cake is one of the best ways of marking such occasions. When you make someone a cake you are not only showing that you appreciate them, but you are giving them some of your time and trouble: a cake personally designed and decorated – however simply or 'unprofessionally' – makes a much more thoughtful present than anything you could buy, and is a lovely centrepiece at a party or family get-together.

When I wrote my first cake book eight years ago I honestly never dreamt anyone would buy it – it was enormous fun to do, but a bit of a family joke, and there was no one more surprised than I was to discover just how many people shared my enthusiasm for decorating cakes and who enjoyed trying out some of my ideas. Over the ensuing years I have naturally made a great many more – including those commissioned by charities, friends and organisations – and I thought it might be time to put down some of these new ideas in another book, together with additional ones specially designed while writing it. As you will see, I have included every sign of the Zodiac, a good standby for birthday cakes if you can't think of any other design.

This is a decorating, not a baking book. I am always more interested in the final look than in the cake within and often use packet cake mixes as my base. I have given a couple of very basic recipes but I leave it up to you to make the cakes as tasty as you like – I shall only help you to make them look good.

I do hope you enjoy these cakes, and that some of them will inspire you to ideas of your own. If you have as much fun making them as I did then it will have been worthwhile.

Finally, just a reminder that the cakes are for special occasions only – we all know the effects of sugar on children's teeth and it's very important that these solidly sweet creations are only consumed a few times a year!

ACKNOWLEDGEMENTS

OWING TO VARIOUS OTHER commitments I found myself having to do this book in something of a rush, and without the help of a wonderful team I would never have been able to design, bake and decorate 39 cakes (yes, there were two ghastly mistakes . . .) in the time. I am deeply grateful to my three special helpers:

My mother Margaret Asher who not only cleared up endlessly and provided sandwiches, coffee and good advice to keep us all going, but who took careful notes about what I was doing and what quantities I used etc., to help me write it all up later.

The brilliant and efficient Sandra Yong, who shopped, baked, iced and decorated tirelessly and without whom the book would not have been possible.

The talented and delightful actress Emma Chambers, who originally came to help wash up, but who was such an excellent pupil that she was soon helping with many of the trickiest decorating jobs.

All the other books I have written have been done entirely at home, but this time my publisher had the wonderful idea of my 'borrowing' a kitchen outside, so that I could fill it with cakes, icing sugar and debris and not have to keep clearing it all away every evening. I was lucky enough to be lent a beautiful new kitchen in one of the show houses in the Chelsea Harbour development by the river in London, and I am very grateful to Globe and to P&O for letting me use it.

I must also thank Kenwood and Magimix, who lent me a food mixer and food processor respectively, both of which proved invaluable (see Equipment, page 17).

Many thanks to Chris Crofton and his assistant Charlie Taylor for so patiently photographing cake after cake, to Patricia Walters for so cleverly designing the book and to Mark Lucas for his usual enthusiastic backing. I am very grateful to Tony Snowdon for photographing the cover so elegantly and for his brilliant spur-of-the-moment jewellery design with my cake cutters and bulldog clips.

Roger Houghton and John Beaton of Pelham Books yet again put up with my being behind on deadlines and gave me support and encouragement far beyond the call of duty.

I would like to thank all the people who have written to me over the years, telling me about their cakes and sometimes sending me pictures – they are always inspiring and it's lovely to know there are so many of you who enjoy cake decorating. Do keep writing.

Lastly, I am very lucky to have a family that puts up with the chaos producing a book inevitably brings (not cake for breakfast *again*, Mum?!) and without their love and inspiration I would have no wish to create cakes in any case.

RECIPES

CAKES

I'm sure you have many tried and tested cake recipes, and you can really use any kind you like for almost all the decorations in this book. If it needs to be shaped then probably a madeira is the best. To calculate how much cake mixture you need use this simple calculation. Fill the cake tin with water, measure it and for each 450ml (¾ pint) make a 1 egg mixture.

BASIC MADEIRA CAKE
To fill a 20cm (8in) round cake tin

225g (8oz) butter or margarine
225g (8oz) caster sugar
4 eggs
225g (8oz) self-raising flour
125g (4oz) plain flour

Mix the two flours together. Cream butter or margarine together with sugar until light and fluffy. Add eggs one at a time, beating well into the mixture and adding a spoonful of flour after each egg. Fold remaining flour into mixture. Turn into a greased and lined tin and level the top. Cook for about 1½ hours in an oven pre-heated to 160°C/325°F/Gas Mark 3 until firm to the touch. Leave for 5 – 10 minutes then turn out and cool on a wire rack.

VARIATIONS

Add grated orange or lemon rind, or replace a tablespoonful of the plain flour with cocoa or coffee powder dissolved in a little warm water.

You may prefer to use fruit cake. It will keep well and is obviously very suitable for Christmas or wedding cakes. Make it ahead of time to let it mature a little.

RICH FRUIT CAKE
To fill a 20cm (8in) round cake tin

250g (8oz) plain flour
pinch of salt
½ teaspoon ground cinnamon
1 teaspoon ground nutmeg
1kg (2lb) mixed fruit
125 g (4oz) shredded almonds
175g (6oz) butter
grated rind ½ lemon
175g (6oz) dark brown sugar
1 tablespoon black treacle
6 eggs
2 tablespoons brandy or rum

Line cake tin with non-stick baking parchment. Sift flour with salt and spices into a mixing bowl and divide this mixture into three portions.

Mix one portion with the fruit and almonds and set aside. Beat the butter until soft, add the lemon rind, sugar and black treacle. Continue beating until the mixture is very soft. Add the eggs, one at a time, beating well between each one, then fold in second portion of the flour mixture. Next mix in the fruit and flour, then the remaining flour mixture and lastly the brandy or rum.

Turn the mixture into the prepared tin and smooth the top. Dip your fingers in warm water and moisten the surface very slightly (this prevents the cake crust from getting hard during the long cooking). Put the cake in the centre of the pre-heated oven at 180°C/350°F/Gas Mark 4 and after one hour reduce the temperature to 160°C/325°F/Gas Mark 3 and cover the top with double thick greaseproof paper or baking parchment. Test after 2 hours with a skewer; when done allow to cool in the tin for about 30 minutes, then turn out onto a rack and leave until quite cold.

Wrap in greaseproof paper or foil and store in an airtight container.

ICINGS

Most of the cakes in this book are decorated with fondant icing, which is extremely easy to use and can be rolled out to cover a cake or modelled with the fingers. You can now buy it ready made in most supermarkets and it really is just as good as homemade and saves a lot of trouble. However, it is obviously more economical to make your own, and the following is a good simple recipe:

FONDANT ICING

450g (1lb) icing sugar
1 egg white★
2 tbsp (30ml) liquid glucose

Warm the glucose to make it easier to spoon out. Mix all the ingredients together in a food processor or by hand until the mixture looks like lumps of breadcrumbs. Turn onto the work surface and knead with the fingers, dusting with icing sugar as necessary to stop it being too sticky. Keep wrapped in clingfilm or in a plastic bag.

When a harder icing is required – such as for the champagne bottle or the Valentine chocolate box – I have recommended using gelatine icing. This is easy to make at home, or you can order packets of ready mix by post (see Addresses, page 19)

GELATINE ICING

450g (1lb) icing sugar
12.5g (½ oz) gelatine powder
4 tbsp (60ml) water
2 tsp (10ml) liquid glucose

Put the water in a heatproof bowl and add the gelatine. Leave to soak for two minutes. Place the bowl in a pan with 1cm (½ in) water and heat gently until the gelatine dissolves. Remove from the heat and stir in the liquid glucose. Allow to cool for two minutes. Turn the mixture into a bowl containing the icing sugar and mix in. If the mixture seems wet add a little more icing sugar until it resembles dough. Wrap in clingfilm or keep in a plastic bag.

Of course a more traditional way of icing cakes is to use royal icing. Many of the cakes in the book can be iced in this way, although it can be tricky to get a really smooth surface. It is also used for the piping of decorations and for sticking pieces of models together.

ROYAL ICING

350g (12oz) icing sugar
1 egg white★

Break the egg white up with a fork and add the icing sugar bit by bit, mixing well after each addition. Add enough to make soft consistency for spreading, stiffer for piping.

WATER ICING

Just add a little water to icing sugar, mixing well, until it is smooth and runny.

You may well want to split some of the cakes and fill them with butter icing. Also you can always stick the fondant onto the cake with a thin layer of butter icing to make it a bit tastier.

BUTTER ICING

225g (8oz) icing sugar
100g (4oz) butter
vanilla essence
15 – 30ml (1 – 2 tbsp) warm water or milk

Cream the butter until soft and gradually beat in the icing sugar, adding a few drops of essence and the milk or water

Orange or lemon

Replace the vanilla essence with a little grated orange or lemon rind and a little of the juice, beating well to avoid curdling the mixture.

Coffee

Replace the vanilla essence with 10ml (2 level tsp) instant coffee powder dissolved in some of the heated liquid.

Chocolate

Either replace 15ml (1 tbsp) of the liquid with 25–40g (1 – 1½oz) melted chocolate, or add 15ml (1 level tbsp) cocoa powder dissolved in a little hot water then cooled.

MARZIPAN

You can make your own if you like, but I really don't think it's worth the trouble. On the whole it's best to use the white type without colouring, but occasionally the yellow can be used to good effect (for the Teddies on page 61 for example).

JAM FOR STICKING

You will need to brush the cakes with jam before covering them with marzipan or fondant. The traditional type is sieved apricot jam, but anything without pips will do. (I have even successfully used redcurrant jelly on occasion). If you warm it first it is easier to use, but it's by no means essential.

★As we are currently advised not to eat raw egg, you may prefer to use dried egg white, adding a little water as directed on the packet.

BASIC TECHNIQUES

Covering a cake with fondant icing

Brush the cake with jam to make it sticky. Dust the work surface well with icing sugar then roll out the fondant icing. Measure the length and height of the side of the cake with a piece of string or tape measure, then cut a piece of icing to fit. Stick it to the cake then trim the top if necessary or other sides if square. Gather up the leftover icing and knead and roll again. Tip the cake upside-down onto the icing and trim round the edge. For oddly shaped cakes you may have to measure several pieces with a tape measure before you fit them onto the cake.

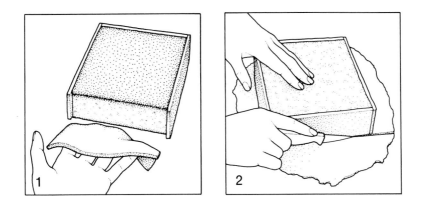

Covering with marzipan

If you are using fruit cakes, you may want to cover them with marzipan first, although even with fruit cake it is not strictly necessary when using fondant, not royal icing. Put the marzipan on in just the same way as for fondant, leaving it a day or so to dry out before icing.

Modelling with fondant

This is just like using plasticine, although you must keep your fingers well dusted with icing sugar, and do always keep the icing wrapped in clingfilm or a plastic bag while you are working, as it will get dry and crusty in the air. Always leave models to dry on non-stick baking parchment.

Colouring fondant

Just knead in drops of food colour bit by bit on the end of a cocktail stick. Wear rubber gloves for the darker colours, or you'll find you walk around looking as if you've just done a murder or cleaned the chimney. I have also discovered while writing this book, that you can knead colour into fondant by using a mixer with the dough hook attached (see Equipment, page 17).

MARCH *PISCES*

PISCES

I HAD ALL SORTS OF ambitious plans to put toffee glass over the sides of this so that it looked like a real tank, but it proved impossible. It was so thick and swirly that you couldn't see the fish at all, which rather defeated the purpose of the whole thing.

EASY WITHOUT FRAME, START AT LEAST TWO DAYS AHEAD IF YOU WANT TO INCLUDE IT – IT CAN BE VERY FIDDLY.

INGREDIENTS
2 26cm (10 ½in) × 13cm (5in) cakes
1kg (2¼ lb) fondant
350g (¾lb) gelatine icing
jam for sticking
icing sugar for rolling
125g (¼lb) royal icing
blue, green, orange and silver food colours

EQUIPMENT
cake board
non-stick baking parchment
paint brush
piping bag with small nozzle

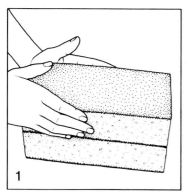

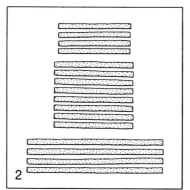

Stick the cakes one on top of the other with jam (or use butter icing if you like) (fig 1). Stand it up on its long side.

Measure the sides and uprights of the cake. Roll out the gelatine icing and cut 8 strips 2cm (1in) higher than the cake, 4 to the width of the cake, and 4 to the length of the cake (fig 2). Let dry on baking parchment for a couple of days.

Keep back a little fondant to make fish, etc. Colour the rest bluey-green. Jam the cake and cover sides and top with rolled out pieces of fondant. Cut fish, weeds, stones out of coloured fondant and stick to tank with a little water or jam. Stick dry tank pieces to cake and to each other with royal icing. When dry paint silver.

MOTHER'S DAY

MOTHER'S DAY

I THINK A LOT OF MUMS would appreciate the joke of being given a sink full of dirty washing-up for their cake – especially if you make sure they don't have to do any *real* washing-up on their special day. If it's a bit too depressingly like real life then you could always make the bowl of roses instead (page 79).

MEDIUM DIFFICULTY.
START COUPLE OF DAYS BEFORE TO LET CROCKERY DRY.

INGREDIENTS
1 cake 23cm × 17cm × 8cm (9in × 6½in × 3in)
jam for sticking
icing sugar for rolling
125g (¼lb) gelatine icing
675g (1½lb) fondant
assorted food colours, including silver
225g (½lb) water icing

EQUIPMENT
dolls' tea-set for moulding
paint brush
non-stick baking parchment

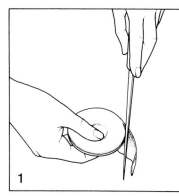

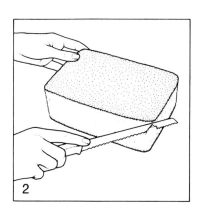

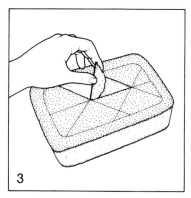

Dust the dolls' tea-set pieces with icing sugar. Roll out the gelatine icing and drape over the pieces, moulding and trimming to fit (fig 1). Leave to dry. Remove carefully. Model taps and knives, forks etc. Leave to dry on baking parchment.

Trim the cake into a sink shape (fig 2).

Mark the bowl with a knife, then score sections and pull them out with the fingers (fig 3).

Jam the cake. Roll out the fondant and drape it over, slashing it so it can fall into the bowl. Line inside of bowl with another piece of fondant (to prevent water icing seeping away) (fig 4).

Paint the taps silver and stick them onto the back of the sink. Paint the crockery and cutlery and when dry position in the bowl. Colour the water icing pale blue and pour it into the sink. Leave to set.

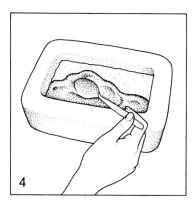

CHAMPAGNE BOTTLE

CHAMPAGNE BOTTLE

T HIS IS REALLY MORE of a surprise centrepiece than a cake. You can fill it with all sorts of delicious mixtures – from strawberries and cream to chocolates – and just break it open at the right moment.

MEDIUM DIFFICULTY.
START SEVERAL DAYS AHEAD.

INGREDIENTS

For bottle
675g (1½lb) gelatine icing
green food colouring
icing sugar for rolling
225g (½lb) cooking chocolate or
chocolate cake covering

For label and foil
rice paper
red food colouring
black food colouring pen
225g (½lb) fondant
gold leaf or gold food colouring

EQUIPMENT
champagne bottle
felt-tip pen or preferably chinagraph pencil
cake board
Blu-Tack or plasticine
plastic bag

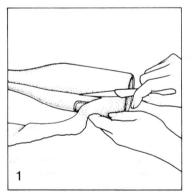

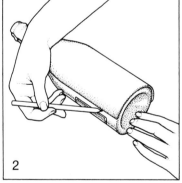

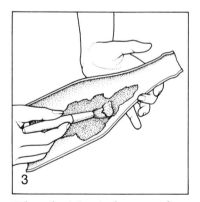

1 Carefully soak the labels off the champagne bottle and keep as templates. Mix green colouring into the icing until it is a good bottle colour. Dust the real bottle liberally with icing sugar. Roll out half of the gelatine icing and drape it over the bottle, then trim to half-way down the sides (fig 1).

2 Wedge the bottle with small pieces of Blu-Tack or plasticine so that it doesn't roll. Mark the bottle where the icing finishes with the felt-tip or chinagraph pencil (fig 2).

3 When the icing is dry enough to move (about 24 hours or less) remove it carefully and make the other half bottle, matching the edges of the icing to the marks on the bottle. Keep left-over scraps in a plastic bag. Let the half bottle dry and remove carefully. Paint the insides of the bottle halves with melted chocolate. This stops the filling making the bottle soggy (fig 3).

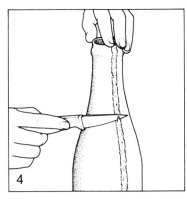

4

Use dampened strips of the left-over gelatine icing to join the halves together, trimming as necessary (fig 4).

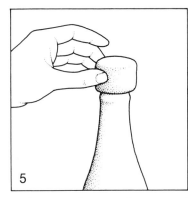

5

Make a cork out of scraps of icing and press onto the top of the bottle (fig 5). Let dry.

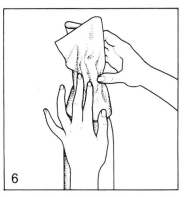

6

Cut labels out of rice paper and decorate with the food colourings. Roll out the 225g (½lb) fondant very thinly and scrunch over the top of the bottle (fig 6).

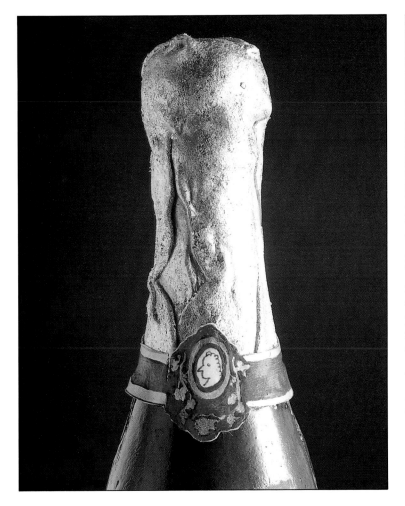

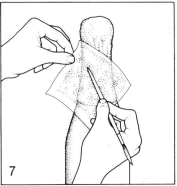

7

Rub the gold leaf onto the icing. This takes time and you have to be very patient (fig 7). Using real gold leaf is very extravagant but for a really special occasion it's worth it. It looks magnificent and is edible. Alternatively paint it with gold colouring, but remember to remove it before eating.

Stick the labels onto the bottle with a little fondant mixed with water. Fill as desired from the bottom.

ARIES

APRIL *ARIES*

THIS COMBINATION OF CUT OUT fondant and piped butter icing gives the Ram a good fleecy look. You could use it for all sorts of other ideas: anything where you wanted a raised, furry texture.

EASY.
START ONE DAY AHEAD.

INGREDIENTS
1 30cm (12in) × 23cm (9in) cake (I used my roasting tin)
675g (1½lb) fondant to cover cake
jam for sticking
icing sugar for rolling
125g (¼lb) fondant for ram
250g (½lb) butter icing
black, yellow and green food colours

EQUIPMENT
black food colouring pen
piping bag with large star nozzle
paper and pencil
cake board

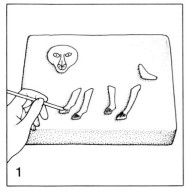

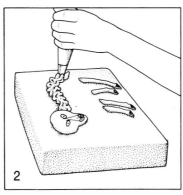

cake, using the paper body to give you an idea where they should go. Add black hooves and features with the food pen (or a brush and black colouring) (fig 1).

Colour the fondant green and cover the cake with it. Draw (or trace from a magazine and enlarge) a ram on a piece of paper and cut it out. Cut the legs, head and tail off so they are separate. Roll out the white fondant and cut out legs, head and tail, using your pieces of paper as templates. Save the scraps of icing to make horns. Position the pieces of fondant on the

Colour the butter icing very pale yellow and put into the piping bag. Pipe the wool, making swirly, shaggy patterns (fig 2).

Colour leftover scraps of fondant black, shape into curly horns and stick to ram's head with a little water. Prop with crumpled kitchen paper so they dry upright (fig 3).

EASTER

I ORIGINALLY MADE THIS CAKE for the third anniversary of the Terry Wogan show. I'd already made him two cakes on previous occasions so I was looking for a new idea. 'What do you think of if I say "Wogan"?' I asked my husband. 'Rabbit, rabbit, rabbit . . .' he replied. So there it was. You obviously needn't make a number if it's for Easter, they would look lovely clustered round any shape of cake.

MEDIUM DIFFICULTY.
START FEW DAYS AHEAD TO GIVE TIME TO MAKE RABBITS.

INGREDIENTS
cake cooked in a large 3 shape
jam for sticking
icing sugar for rolling
675g (1½lb) fondant
450g (1lb) royal icing
pink food colour
1.8kg (4lb) fondant to make rabbits

EQUIPMENT
large round cake board
piping bag with shell and No 2 nozzles
non-stick baking parchment

EASTER

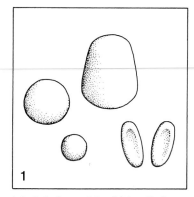

1

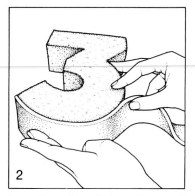

2

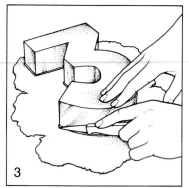

3

Model about 34 rabbits (!) from the fondant (fig 1). Let them dry on the baking parchment.

Jam the sides of the cake. Roll out about two-thirds of the fondant and cut strips to cover the sides (fig 2).

Cover the top of the cake by turning it upside down onto the rolled out icing, or by using the cake tin as a template (fig 3).

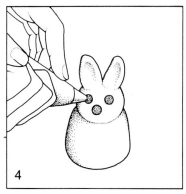

4

Colour the royal icing pink. Pipe shell pattern round the top of the cake. Pipe features onto the rabbits (fig 4) and then paint the insides of ears pink. Position rabbits round cake.

FIRST FOLIO

FIRST FOLIO

I FIRST MADE THIS last year for the inauguration of the rebuilding of Shakespeare's Globe theatre on the South Bank. It was Shakespeare's birthday (April 23rd) and Dame Judi Dench dug the first hole with a huge JCB and then fireworks and water cannons were let off. It was all very exciting and I think Will would have been very proud.

It's unlikely you will want to celebrate such a relatively obscure anniversary but I thought it would show you how effective a book can look if you trace a fairly intricate design onto it. This is a very large cake, but you could easily scale it down.

MEDIUM DIFFICULTY.
START SEVERAL DAYS AHEAD, DEPENDING ON THE DESIGN YOU CHOOSE.

INGREDIENTS	EQUIPMENT
2 large rectangular sponge cakes	*picture for tracing*
(mine were 25cm×20cm (10in×8in)	*tracing paper*
jam for sticking	*(I used baking parchment, as I had some anyway)*
icing sugar for rolling	*pencil*
1.8kg (4lb) gelatine icing	*food colouring pen*
(you can use ordinary fondant, but the gelatine icing	*large cake board or piece of hardboard*
dries harder and so is easier to draw on)	*paint brush*
red and gold food colours or gold leaf	

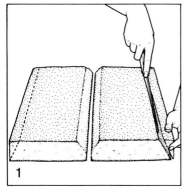

1

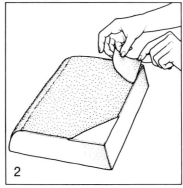

2

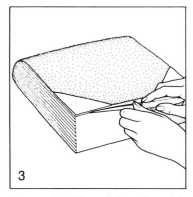

3

(These cakes are so large, you may want to split them and fill with butter icing first.) Trim both cakes into a book shape (fig. 1).

Work on one cake at a time. Roll out a small amount of the icing, jam the corners of the cake then cover with icing (fig 2).

Cover the sides of the cake with icing, then mark pages quickly by drawing a knife along (fig 3).

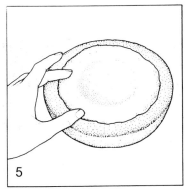

5

Stick a mound of marzipan to top of crab body to round it (fig 5).

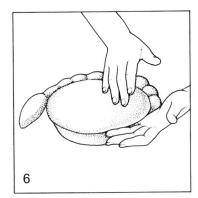

6

Cover sides of body. Cover top, leaving a lip extending over the edge (fig 6).

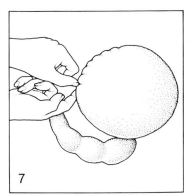

7

Crimp edge of shell with fingers (fig 7).

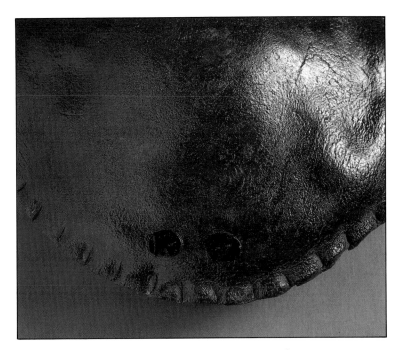

Cut two little liquorice eyes and stick in position. Put crab on board and stick claws to body with a little fondant or jam. With sponge dab on yellow and brown colouring to give speckled effect. Brush him with a little glycerine water to make him shiny if you like.

PLATE OF SPAGHETTI

PLATE OF SPAGHETTI

THIS VERY SILLY CAKE IS easy and quick to do, and as pasta is so popular with children nowadays I think it would make a good birthday cake. I've moulded the plate out of icing, but you could just as well put it on a real plate if you haven't time. The spaghetti looks fine without sauce (*al burro?*) but I've added 'Neapolitan sauce and parmesan' to finish it off. I found a strawberry pie filling which looks pretty good, but you might find an even more tomatoey-looking sweet sauce; let me know if you do.

EASY.
START TWO DAYS BEFORE IF YOU WANT AN ICING PLATE,
OR SAME DAY IF YOU USE A REAL ONE.

INGREDIENTS

For plate
225g (1/2lb) gelatine icing
icing sugar for rolling
green food colour

For spaghetti
1 18cm (7in) sandwich sponge
225g (1/2lb) butter icing
225g (1/2lb) royal icing
yellow or brown food colours
strawberry fruit filling
ground almonds

EQUIPMENT
real plate for moulding or using
piping bag and No 4 plain nozzle
paint brush
cake board

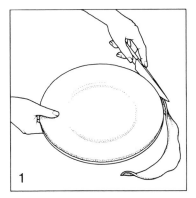

1

Dust the plate well with corn-flour. Roll out the gelatine paste and cover the plate, trimming neatly round the edge with a sharp knife (fig 1).

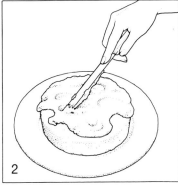

2

Let the plate dry well, for about 12 hours, then remove and paint a pattern round the edge. Put the cake onto the plate (icing or real) and spread with the butter icing, coloured cream (fig 2).

3

Colour the royal icing cream, then pipe all over the cake until it looks like spaghetti (fig 3).

Add fruity 'tomato sauce' and ground almonds 'parmesan' if desired.

THE SWIMMER

THE SWIMMER

T HE IMAGE OF THE British holidaymaker is never very glamorous but I'm quite fond of this happy chap, although I am rather worried about his colour now we know what terrible damage the sun does to our pale, sensitive skins . . .

MEDIUM DIFFICULTY.
START TWO DAYS BEFORE.

INGREDIENTS
I SPHERICAL CAKE APPROX 12CM (5IN) DIAMETER
(I COOKED MINE IN A CHRISTMAS PUDDING TIN, BUT A
PUDDING BASIN CAKE WOULD DO JUST AS WELL).
1 mini roll
icing sugar for rolling
jam for sticking
350g (¾lb) marzipan
675g (1½lb) fondant
pink, blue and red food colours

EQUIPMENT
cake board
paint brush
non-stick baking parchment

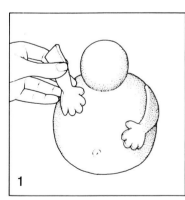

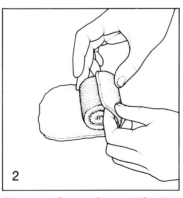

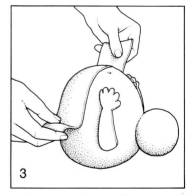

Cover the cake with marzipan to give it support. Let dry a little. Colour three-quarters fondant pink. Cover the cake with pink fondant then roll a head and stick it on with a little water or jam. Mark a 'tummy button'. Roll and cut two arms and stick them on (fig 1).

Cut two feet and set aside. Let all dry on baking parchment for 12 hours or so. Cut the mini roll in half and roll each half in marzipan (fig 2). Cover with pink fondant and let dry for 12 hours or so.

Cut a strip of white fondant and stick to lower half of body (fig 3).

THE SWIMMER

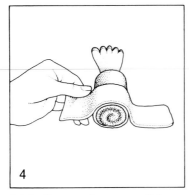

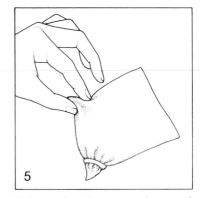

Stick feet to bottom of legs. Cover top of legs with white fondant (fig 4).

Paint red stripes onto legs and body. Stick body onto legs. Roll and cut a square 'handkerchief'. Pinch the corners, then add tiny strips to look like knots (fig 5).

Stick handkerchief onto head. Add a little fondant nose. Paint nose, cheeks and mouth red and eyes blue.

CROCODILE

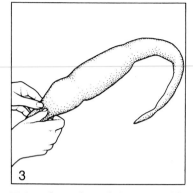

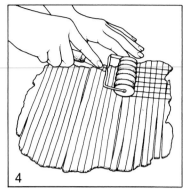

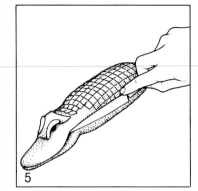

3

Trim the sides of the crocodile but leave the surplus at each end – join any spare icing with the half you kept back. Shape a long tail from the surplus icing. Mould the icing over the doughnut head and shape a snout from the surplus (fig 3).

4

Roll out half the remaining icing and cut squares, using a rolling mosaic cutter or any other suitable device (or a knife if necessary) (fig 4).

5

Damp the cake and stick the squares all over the back and head. Mark the features with a knife (fig 5).

Mould legs from remaining icing. Stick to crocodile with water. Add little balls of icing for eyes. Paint them black. Pipe tiny teeth with royal icing (or use broken nuts). Glaze him with glycerine water.

ROSE BOWL

VIRGO

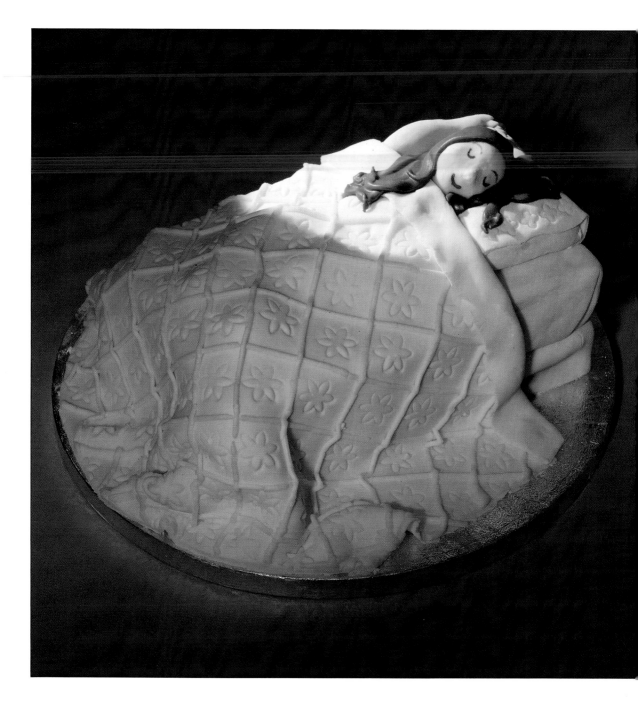

SEPTEMBER *VIRGO*

T HIS ISN'T AN EASY star sign to portray without causing undue giggles. I decided a beautiful young girl alone in her bed sleeping peacefully between virginal white sheets would sum it up quite well (of course what you and I don't know is that there is probably a handsome icing prince hiding under the bed . . .)

MEDIUM DIFFICULTY.
START TWO DAYS AHEAD.

INGREDIENTS
cake baked in a tray about 22cm × 33cm (9in × 13in)
jam for sticking
icing sugar for rolling
900g (2lb) fondant
225g (½lb) white marzipan
225g (½lb) royal icing
pink and brown food colours

EQUIPMENT
small and tiny flower cutters to make patterns
piping bag with No 2 and flat ribbon nozzles
non-stick baking parchment
1 30cm (12in) cake board

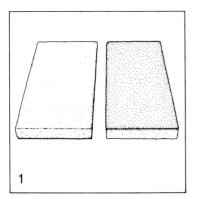

1

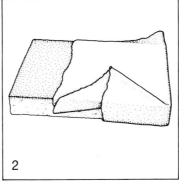

2

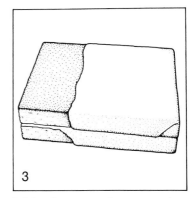

3

Trim cake and cut in half lengthways (fig 1).

Jam top of one piece of cake. Roll out about a quarter of the fondant and cover most of the cake. Ice the other piece of cake in exactly the same way but make 'envelope corners' as shown (fig 2).

Stick the two pieces together with jam (fig 3). Stick to the cake board with a little icing.

VIRGO

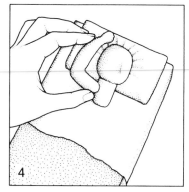

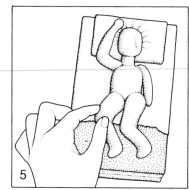

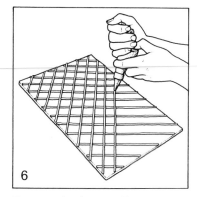

Mould a little pillow out of marzipan. Cover it with fondant then mark a few creases with a knife and some patterns with the tiny flower cutter. Stick it onto the bed with a little water. Colour a small amount of fondant pale pink, then model a head and arm and stick them to the pillow (fig 4).

Roughly model the rest of the body from marzipan and stick it to the bed (fig 5).

Keeping back a small amount to make the top sheet, roll out the remainder of the fondant on a piece of baking parchment. Measure over the bed with a piece of string, allowing extra for 'drape' then cut the fondant to size. Working quickly, pipe lattice pattern with the royal icing and No 2 nozzle (fig 6). Again working quickly so the lattice doesn't dry out and break, add patterns with flower cutter.

Drape the cover quickly over the bed, making folds with your fingers and trimming edges as necessary. Touch up any broken lattice work. Roll out the remaining fondant and cut a narrow strip. Tuck over top of 'bedspread'. Colour small amount of royal icing brown and pipe hair using the ribbon nozzle. Paint eyes and mouth.

SCHOOLBOY

SCHOOLBOY

MY SEVEN-YEAR-OLD SON calmly announced one day last year that 'we have to take a special cake to school tomorrow for the end of term party'. Help! I rushed round the corner to my local shop and bought a jam sandwich and a doughnut and made him this schoolboy cake – it was a great hit with his classmates. I've adapted it here for going back to school, but it would make a lovely birthday cake or for any school occasion.

EASY.
START DAY BEFORE.

INGREDIENTS
1 20cm (8in) round cake
1 doughnut
675g (1½lb) fondant
225g (½lb) royal icing
icing sugar for rolling
jam for sticking
green and red food colours

EQUIPMENT
cake board
piping bag with Nos 1 and 3 nozzles

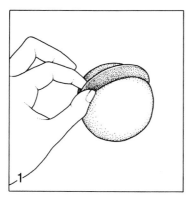

Level the top of the cake or use the underneath. Jam the cake and use about two-thirds of the fondant to drape over. Colour a small amount of fondant pink then cover the doughnut with it. Colour small amount of fondant green, and cover the top of his head. Stick the head onto the cake. Cut out a little peak from green fondant and stick upright onto cap, holding with the fingers until it is dry enough to stand up (fig 1).

Cut a tie from green fondant and stick below head. Cut two white triangular pieces to make the collar. Cut out tiny badge shape and stick to cap. Roll a little round nose from pink fondant and attach to face. Pipe eyes and mouth with No 3 nozzle and white stripes on tie with No 1. Colour remaining royal icing red, then pipe stripes onto tie, badge details and writing on cake (fig 2).

SING A SONG OF SIXPENCE